WS

Please return/renew this item by the last date shown

worcestershire
c o u n t y c o u n c i l
Libraries & Learning

700036197924

D1438812

For Erica Wakerly

First published 2009 by Walker Books Ltd
87 Vauxhall Walk, London SE11 5HJ

2 4 6 8 10 9 7 5 3 1

© 2009 Polly Dunbar

The right of Polly Dunbar to be identified as author/illustrator
of this work has been asserted by her in accordance with
the Copyright, Designs and Patents Act 1988.

This book has been typeset in Gill Sans MT Schoolbook.

Printed in China.

All rights reserved. No part of this book may be reproduced,
transmitted or stored in an information retrieval system in any
form or by any means, graphic, electronic or mechanical,
including photocopying, taping and recording, without prior
written permission from the publisher.

British Library Cataloguing in Publication Data:
a catalogue record for this book is available
from the British Library.

ISBN 978-1-4063-0908-9

www.walker.co.uk

Tilly and
her friends
all live
together in
a little yellow
house...

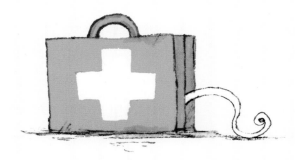

Doodle
Bites

Polly Dunbar

WALKER BOOKS
AND SUBSIDIARIES
LONDON · BOSTON · SYDNEY · AUCKLAND

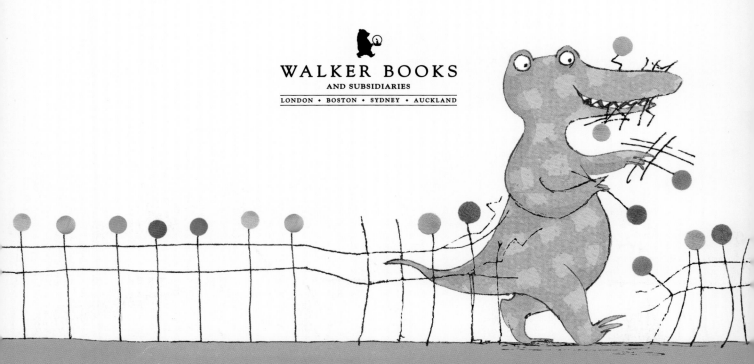

Doodle

woke up

feeling

BITEY!

After she had CHOMpED her breakfast,

she CHEWED the post.

She even CRUNCHED and

MUNCHED the sofa.

While she was **NIBBLING** the lamp,

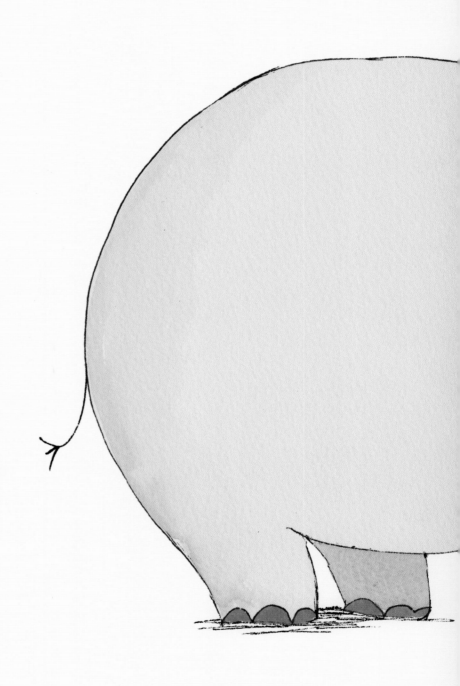

Doodle spied something very good to bite.

"OW!"

shouted Tumpty.

"That's my
bottom!"

Tumpty was very upset.

"You shouldn't bite your friends," said Tilly. "It's not nice."

"Mmm,"
said Doodle.

BITEY! BITEY!

So Tumpty stamped on Doodle's tail.

"YOW!"

shouted Doodle.

"That's my tail!"

"You shouldn't stamp on your friends," said Tilly, "even if they bite you.

"It's not nice."

Tumpty was crying.

Doodle was

crying.

Even Hector started crying.

"Don't worry, I'm here!" said Pru,
and she gave Tumpty an
extra-large plaster
for his bottom.

Tilly gave Doodle
a bandage for
her tail.

Hector
and Tiptoe
got plasters too.

Then
Pru kissed
everyone
better.

Even Doodle!

"I'm sorry
I stamped
on your tail,"
said Tumpty.

"I'm sorry
I bit your
bottom,"
said Doodle.

Hurray!
Everyone was happy again!

But Doodle still felt just a little bit bitey!

"Oh no you don't!"
laughed
Tumpty.

Pru gave Doodle an
extra-special
bandage.

No more bitey bitey!

The End